DEADLY DRIVE

Justine Fontes

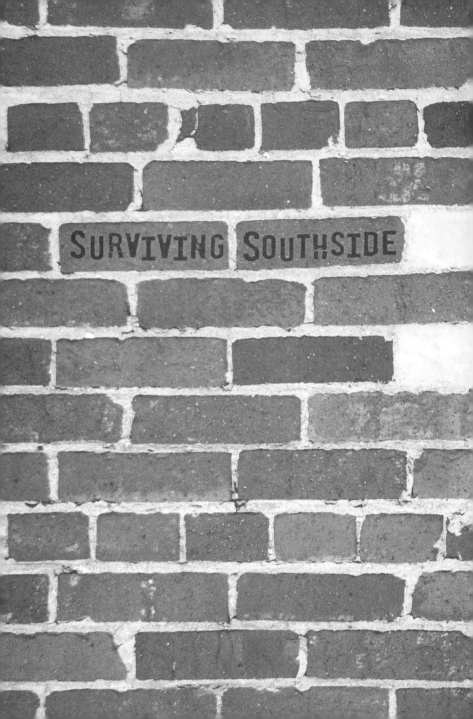

SURVIVING SOUTHSIDE

Deadly Drive

Justine Fontes

MINNEAPOLIS

Darby Creek
A division of Lerner Publishing Group, Inc.
241 First Avenue North
Minneapolis, MN 55401 U.S.A.

Website address: www.lernerbooks.com

The images in this book are used with the permission of: © Image Source/Getty Images, (main image) front cover; © iStockphoto .com/Jill Fromer, (banner background) front cover and throughout interior; © iStockphoto.com/Naphtalina, (brick wall background) front cover and throughout interior.

Main body text set in Janson Text LT Std 55 Roman 12/17.5.
Typeface provided by Adobe Systems.

Library of Congress Cataloging-in-Publication Data

Fontes, Justine.
    Deadly drive / by Justine Fontes.
        pages   cm. — (Surviving Southside)
        ISBN 978-1-4677-0310-9 (lib. bdg. : alk. paper)
        [1. Drunk driving—Fiction. 2. Dating (Social customs)—
    Fiction. 3. High schools—Fiction. 4. Schools—Fiction.
    5. Mexican Americans—Fiction.] I. Title.
    PZ7.F73576De 2013
    [Fic]—dc23   2012027177

Manufactured in the United States of America
1 – BP – 12/31/12

To Officer Daniel Scott Gabriel Murray and all the other brave police officers and EMTs who face the consequences of drunk driving; Kese Smith, Media Relations, Houston Police Department; and Donna Hawkins, Houston District Attorney's Office. Thanks for sharing your expertise!
—J.F.

CHAPTER 1

Sometimes I think I must be the oldest virgin at Southside High School. But I hope to change that soon! My name is Roberto Ramirez. Everyone calls me Rob.

I'm a seventeen-year-old senior. I've got lots of friends at school, and girls tell me I'm pretty good looking. But I've never had a real girlfriend.

My best friend, Adam, says it's because I'm too shy. Maybe that's true.

I think I might have finally met the right girl, though. Gabi Montoya transferred to Southside High this year from St. Michael's. Too bad her family is so strict. We haven't had that much time alone together.

I'm not going to say I'm in love. Still, I can't get Gabi out of my mind! Her hair is perfect. Her eyes are more than perfect. It's not just that they're this dark, intense brown. They also seem to shine whenever she smiles.

Gabi's one of the smartest people I've ever met too. She aces all her classes, but she isn't stuck up about it.

The best part is, I think she's really into me. She just seems kind of shy, like I am. Gabi isn't like all the other girls at Southside. She seems sort of pure. Old fashioned, even. I'm crazy for these plaid skirts she wears. I could watch her pull up her knee socks all day long!

Unfortunately, it's almost time for class. Everyone else rushes up and down the hall. Lockers bang open and closed all around me. I stand in front of mine like a lovesick zombie as Gabi strolls away.

Adam nudges me with his elbow. "Dude! You're staring again." He laughs. "You have got it bad!"

Adam and I have been friends for so long that I can't remember ever not knowing him. So I don't care if he knows I'm crazy for Gabi.

"I hate to see you suffering, man," he says. "Why don't you just go for it? Girls get horny too, you know. Gabi's probably waiting for you to make a move."

I shrug. He's my friend, but I'm a little sick of hearing about how many times he's hooked up with his girlfriend, Vera. Since they got serious last month, Adam hasn't stopped bragging about it.

"Hey, I have a plan!" Adam says. "Why don't you, me, Vera, and Gabi sneak out at lunch on Wednesday?"

The four of us have study hall together right after lunch on Wednesdays. And our afternoons are pretty light.

"Remember that patch of woods I told you about?" Adam adds. "We could all go there for a picnic. It's not far from school. We'd be back in time for eighth period."

I remember hearing about the woods. Adam went on and on about him and Vera having this amazing time under the trees after school last week. He gushed, "I thought sex was great inside. But out in the open . . . it's like you're one with nature. Like even the birds are cheering you on."

I shrug. "That sounds cool. I wonder if Gabi will go for it."

Adam knows I've never skipped a class in my whole life. I'd never risk messing up my soccer scholarship.

Gabi's even more of a straight arrow than I am. She already has several scholarships lined up. She plans to study premed at college, then go to medical school right after.

Adam grins his sly, charming grin. "You'll never get anywhere if you don't try."

"I guess it wouldn't hurt to ask."

"Why don't you bring along some insurance," Adam says. "Girls really loosen up with liquor. I never would have gotten into

Vera's pants without a little help from my man Jack Daniels."

Adam knows I can get booze. I've brought some to a couple of parties. My parents hardly drink, but we have a cabinet full of booze because my dad's a mail carrier. At Christmas, customers are always giving him cookies or bottles of nice liquor. He puts away the booze and forgets about it unless we have company. It isn't hard to sneak out a bottle now and then.

Adam smiles. "This is going to be the best picnic ever!"

I slap his hand high and low. I'm so excited I almost go to the wrong class. What if Gabi says yes? What if we really do take things to the next level? Kissing her has been amazing. I can't even imagine going all the way . . .

As soon as class is over, I race down the hall to catch Gabi before next period. I tell her Adam's picnic plan.

She looks skeptical. "Do you think we'll get caught?"

"Not if we get back on time for last period." Then I wink and say, "What's the point of being a senior if you can't have a little fun?"

Gabi looks thoughtful. "How will we get there?"

"Won't you have the SUV?"

Gabi's only had her driver's license for a little while. Her parents have been letting her drive their old car to school. She's been bragging about driving almost as much as Adam's been bragging about having sex with Vera.

Gabi smiles. "It *would* be fun to use the car for a picnic instead of just school and errands."

"We won't be going far," I add.

Gabi's dark eyes twinkle with mischief. "You're right! Why shouldn't we have a little fun?"

Then she presses her lips against mine and everything else vanishes. I forget we're standing in a crowded hall with students pushing past us. My heart pounds under my T-shirt. Can Gabi feel it? I press closer to her and feel her heart beating almost as fast as mine!

How will I ever wait until Wednesday?

CHAPTER 2

I can't focus on anything, not even soccer practice. All my teammates are saying, "Rob, get your head in the game!"

Benito teases me. "Earth to Rob! Come in Rob!"

I'm lucky we're only practicing, not playing another school.

At the dinner table Tuesday night, my family teases me too.

Dad shouts, *"Hijo! Estas aquí?"*

I look up and realize everyone's staring at me.

My younger brother Luis laughs. "Berto isn't here. He's with his girlfriend, *Gab*-eee."

When he says her name, Luis flutters his eyelashes and simpers. I want to smack him. Instead, I just blush.

Mom grins. "Pass Luis the salt already. He's been asking for ten minutes."

I try to "stay in the game" for the rest of dinner. But it isn't easy. I keep thinking about the picnic in the woods with Gabi. What if she lets me get to second base—or even third?

I don't dare to hope things'll go that fast. Still, I can't help dreaming.

"*Hijo!*" Dad shouts. "If you don't help with the dishes, Luis is going to eat your dessert."

I can't let that happen. Mom made flan!

I scramble to get the plates off the table. After dessert, everyone else goes into the den to watch TV.

I tell them I'm going to my room to do some homework. On the way, I open the liquor cabinet and grab a pint bottle of Southern Comfort. It's small enough to hide in my backpack. I cushion it with my soccer clothes so the bottle won't break. Then I start some homework before my mind drifts back to Gabi's legs, eyes, lips, hair, voice . . .

As soon as I get on the bus the next morning, Adam asks, "Did you bring the insurance?"

I unzip my pack and push aside the clothes so he can see the bottle.

He grins. "Perfect! I brought some soda for mixers."

I close my pack and say, "It's going to be a long morning."

Adam nods. "And a great afternoon!"

We high and low five.

As expected, the morning crawls by as slow as a slug. Gabi sits near me in third period trig. She catches me glancing at her, and then neither one of us can look away.

Suddenly something blocks the view, a wall of blue fabric. I look up and realize Mrs. Harris is standing between us. She's tall, strict, and always wears blue. Everyone laughs, except Mrs. Harris. When she frowns, she looks like one of those ugly statues they put on buildings to scare away evil spirits.

Gabi looks even prettier when she blushes. I have to force myself to look at the blackboard instead.

After an eternity, the bell rings. It's lunchtime!

As we had arranged, Gabi and I meet Adam and Vera outside the cafeteria. Then Adam makes a dash for it, pulling Vera along by the hand. We run for the car, mostly for fun. Our school has an open campus for juniors and seniors, so everyone with a car usually leaves during their lunch period anyway. Gabi's long, dark hair floats behind her as she runs.

We scramble into the SUV, breathless from running. Gabi buckles her safety belt and waits until we all buckle ours. She signals, even though no one's watching. Then she pulls out of the parking lot. I look over my shoulder. We're free!

Adam laughs. "Relax, man. It's not a jailbreak."

"For all anyone knows, we're just leaving for lunch," Vera points out.

I feel excited and just a little scared. Gabi seems jumpy too. I wonder if she's ever cut class before. The air conditioner's broken, so all the windows are open. Her hair dances in the breeze.

Adam tells her where to turn. Soon we're on this little back road I never knew existed. Weeds poke out of the pavement.

"Keep going straight for a while," Adam says.

Gabi nods. Her eyes leave the road just long enough to meet mine. I smile. Gabi blushes. This is going to be so great!

Gabi turns on the radio, and we sing along for a few minutes. Then Adam says, "Turn here and park."

At first I don't even see the dirt road. But Gabi does, and she turns and parks the SUV. It doesn't look very scenic—more like an abandoned lot than some romantic woods.

Then we walk for a few minutes, and it's just as nice as Adam promised.

"This is awesome!" I shout.

Adam grins. "We were going to keep this place as our little secret, but . . ."

Vera punches his arm. "But Mr. Bigmouth had to tell his best bro."

"I thought you liked my big mouth," Adam says. He slides his hand around the back of Vera's neck and plunges his tongue into her mouth.

Gabi looks away until they finish kissing.

"Sorry about that," Adam laughs. "We can't seem to keep our hands off each other."

"Or our tongues," Vera says.

I laugh too, and Gabi joins in. But she seems a little embarrassed.

Adam opens his backpack. He spreads out a sheet on the ground. Then he says, "Rob brought a special treat. Either of you girls ever tasted Southern Comfort?"

Vera sits down on the sheet and asks, "Is it as good as Jack Daniels?"

Adam sits down beside her. "Much sweeter. I think you'll like it even better. And I brought some sodas to mix."

Gabi says, "I can't drink. I'll be driving us back."

I sigh. So much for the insurance. But I'm not really surprised. Gabi's family is super strict. They go to church every Sunday, not just on holidays like my parents.

"Come on," Adam says. "You won't be driving for hours."

Vera teases, "What are you, some kind of prude?"

Gabi blushes. I figure she must be a virgin too. But then she shocks us all by grabbing the bottle and taking a big swig like it's nothing! She wipes her pretty mouth and says, "I've been sneaking out of my house since I was fourteen."

Vera's mouth drops open. "Wow!"

Adam adds some liquor to his soda. Gabi takes another pull from the bottle. Then she says, "The trick is to look like Mommy's good girl. And if you get caught, cry real pretty and say, 'I've never done anything like this before—I swear!'"

Vera cracks up. "I thought you were some prissy good girl. But you're all right!'"

Gabi grins this sly, sexy grin I've never seen before.

Vera takes the bottle from Gabi and toasts, "To getting away with everything!"

Adam raises his cup of soda. Vera pours some booze into mine. And we all drink to that.

The Southern Comfort makes the cola

taste funny. But it goes down pretty smooth.

"Try it straight," Gabi suggests.

I tip the bottle to my lips and take a tiny sip. It's so strong I cough and sputter. Everyone laughs, even me.

We keep "sweetening" our sodas for a while, except for Gabi. She drinks straight from the bottle.

I'm glad Dad doesn't like the stuff. At the rate we're going, there won't be anything to bring home. If we were back at Southside, lunch would just be ending, and the bottle's almost empty!

Adam suddenly lets out this huge *buuurrrrp*! We laugh so hard I almost pee my pants.

I stand up too fast and fall down on all fours! I stay there till the world stops spinning. Then I go behind a tree.

At first I feel too embarrassed to pee, knowing the girls are close enough to hear me. Then I hear my three friends laughing, talking, and burping. So I just let it fly. The sun, wind, and chirping birds all add to this giddy feeling of freedom, like we're escaped convicts reveling in the open sky.

CHAPTER 3

Pretty soon Vera's slurring her words. She tells Adam, "You look handsomer when I'm drunk." Then she giggles. "Is that even a word, *handsomer*?"

"Maybe you mean hotter," Gabi says. And her dark eyes lock on mine. I feel like I'm falling into them, and I want to stay there forever.

She finally breaks the gaze, and I realize she's looking at my lips. This is it!

Adam grabs Vera's hand and says, "Come

on!" He starts running into the woods, pulling Vera along. Giggling, she stumbles, falls, and drags Adam down with her. They roll on the grass, laughing, then kissing.

Gabi and I stare at them until it gets so R-rated we have to look away. I know this is the moment. I lean close. I want to make this the best kiss she's ever had. But suddenly I'm nervous. Gabi's been sneaking out since she was fourteen . . . will she be able to tell I'm a virgin? Will she laugh at me if I don't do it right?

She leans in to meet me, so close I can smell her shampoo. And then I don't care about anything else. I'm going for it. Our lips meet, and the feeling is totally intense.

Before long we're making out on the blanket. Her warm breath in my ear drives me crazy. I sneak my hand up her skirt. She doesn't push me away.

Her thighs feel cool and smooth. How far will she let me go?

I open my eyes to see Gabi's face. Is she as into this as I am? Her eyes are closed, and she makes this sort of shuddery moan.

I can't believe we're really going to do this! I realize I better bum a condom off Adam. No way do I want to get Gabi pregnant! And I know that can happen—just last year, this guy Luke got his girlfriend pregnant the first time they had sex. Everyone at Southside was talking about it.

I'm so hot I can barely breathe. Just as I'm wondering if I should get up, Adam and Vera walk over to us, deliberately making a lot of noise. Adam even says, "Ahem." We all crack up. The moment is over.

Vera points to her watch. "We better hurry. It's almost time for last period."

Gabi jumps up and brushes the leaves off her clothes.

CHAPTER 4

On the way back to the car, Gabi stumbles. I'm not totally steady either, but I manage to catch her before she falls. We walk the rest of the way with our arms around each other. I love the way it feels to have her hip pressed against mine.

But then I wonder: is she leaning on me because she wants to stay close, or is she too drunk to walk a straight line?

"You okay to drive?" I ask.

Gabi hesitates.

Adam pops the top off a soda. "Here, the caffeine will keep you alert."

Gabi chugs it till foam runs out between her lips. She wipes her mouth, then drinks some more. "Thanks."

She glances at her reflection in the side-view mirror. "Yikes!" She grabs a brush out of her purse. I watch her run it down her beautiful hair. Her big eyes find mine, and I want to kiss her again. But we really have to go!

Gabi fishes the keys out of her purse, then drops them in the dirt. I pick them up and say, "I didn't drink as much as you. Do you want me to drive?"

Gabi shakes her head. "You don't even have your license yet."

I roll my eyes. "Jeez! Just because I messed up the parallel parking."

Everyone laughs.

Gabi opens the door and bounces into the driver's seat. She shouts, "Let's go! Let's go!"

Vera and Adam scramble into the back. I jump into the passenger's seat and buckle my seat belt.

I can't help thinking about the driver's ed. lesson about drunk driving. It doesn't take much alcohol to mess up your judgment or slow down your reflexes. But what choice do we have? If I call a cab, we're bound to be late for class and get in trouble for leaving school. Gabi's parents would ground her. They probably wouldn't let her see me again either.

Maybe Gabi can tell I'm worried.

"I'll take it slow," she says. "It's not like we're on the highway full of cops."

Adam agrees. "It's a quiet back road. Just be careful."

Gabi nods and starts the engine. She doesn't signal to get back onto the road. But it's not like she's taking her driver's test, and we're the only ones in sight. It almost feels like we're the only people in the world.

The SUV weaves a little bit. But mostly Gabi manages to stay in the right lane and well under the speed limit. Vera and Adam start kissing. I turn on the radio to cover the smacking sounds.

Vera breaks the kiss long enough to say,

"Ooh! I love this song. Turn it up!"

The windows are all the way down and it's hard to hear over the wind, so I crank the radio to the max. Vera unclicks her belt to climb onto Adam's lap. I glance back and see his hand move up her thigh.

I turn back to look at the road. It won't be much longer now. I tell Gabi, "We should probably go in through a back door. We don't want anyone asking for a study hall pass and smelling our breath. "

She nods. "We can use the one near the girl's gym. There's never any teachers near there."

I wonder if she's thinking what I'm thinking: that every week has a Wednesday, and we should do this again really soon!

I'm about to say so when Gabi gasps. An armadillo's crawling along at the edge of the road. Its armor is great against coyotes and other animals. But it doesn't stand a chance against an SUV.

Gabi stomps on the brakes and turns the wheel sharply. I want to say, "Don't!" But it's too late. I only get as far as opening my mouth before the car jolts onto the sandy shoulder.

Gabi panics. She yanks the wheel back. But the shoulder is steep, and instead of regaining the road, the car flips.

Seconds pass with strange slowness. My stomach heaves as the SUV rolls all the way over and then lands on its wheels. Vera's shrill shriek ends abruptly.

Adam screams, "No!"

Something white punches me in the face. I realize it's the airbag rocketing out of the glove compartment with a big poof. Through the corner of my eye, I see Gabi's bag puff out too.

I turn my head to see what's happened to Vera and Adam. Pain grips my neck like a pit bull biting a rat. The sting only lets up a little when I turn my head back to face front. In that brief glance, I've seen something I will never forget.

CHAPTER 5

"Oh my God!" Adam screams.

Gabi says nothing—just stares out her side window. She's seeing what I glimpsed: Vera's bloody body sprawled on the ground. Vera's head is cracked open, bloody lumps of brain spilled out on the ground beside it. They look like something you'd see in a big jar on *CSI*.

No one has to take a pulse to know Vera is dead. No surgery, no stitches, not even a medical miracle can fix that.

Adam opens his door and pukes. As soon as the smell reaches me, I want to puke too. I fight back the rising bile—I know if I bend over, my neck will hurt even more, and I don't want to pass out.

While I try to focus on not puking, something else grabs my attention. My nausea and my neck suddenly don't seem so bad once I see the bloody mess that used to be my knee. Banging into the gearshift must have screwed it up bad. I shout, "Call 9-1-1!"

Gabi stares straight ahead like she's made of stone. She doesn't seem injured. She's just gone from shock.

In spite of the pain gripping my neck, I look back at Adam. I don't see any blood on him. But like Gabi, he stares blankly forward.

I realize neither one of them is in any condition to get help. It hurts to reach in my back pocket, but I do it anyway.

My phone's screen is cracked! The impact pushed me so hard against the seat that I must've crushed it. So I grab Gabi's purse. I fumble around, finding a hairbrush, a tampon, breath mints, and finally her cell phone.

The dispatcher answers quickly. "9-1-1, what is your emergency?"

"Car wreck. We need an ambulance and . . ." It's hard to even say the words. ". . . someone's dead."

"Where are you?"

I feel like an idiot. Where are we? I don't know the name of the road. I do my best to describe the location. "We were on our way to Southside High School. It's an old road . . ."

"Would that be the access road near . . ."

Her voice sounds calm and experienced. She mentions a street name I don't recognize. Then she tells me they are tracking the signal from Gabi's phone and that help will arrive soon. I feel the hot blood running down my leg. I'm so scared it's hard to breathe.

The dispatcher asks me my name and about any injuries. As soon as I tell her my last name, I think, "Oh God! Dad's going to kill me!"

I describe what happened, though I leave out that we were drinking. Mom's gonna completely freak out, I realize. She fusses when I get a bruise playing soccer. What will she do when she sees my knee?

The dispatcher wonders about the other passengers in the vehicle. I don't want to say that Vera is dead again, so I ask Gabi and Adam, "Are you guys okay?"

Gabi blinks but doesn't say anything.

Adam groans. "My shoulder and chest hurt from the belt, but I'm . . . okay."

He doesn't sound okay. He sounds even more scared than I am.

With the pit bull gnawing on my neck, I don't want to turn my head. But I need to know if Gabi is hurt. I repeat her name. "Gabi! Gabrielle!"

She turns to me. Her eyes are two empty pits of fear.

"Are you okay?" I ask slowly and loudly, hoping to break through her shock.

"My arms hurt," she mutters.

"But you're okay?"

She doesn't answer.

I tell the dispatcher that they seem all right. She says that help in on the way.

Then Adam leans forward and suddenly notices my knee. "Dude. Your leg is messed up . . ."

I wince. "Tell me about it."

Through the mass of blood, I can see bits of white bone. Will I ever play soccer again? What will happen to my college scholarship?

Gabi sees the blood and bone, and her pale face turns even paler.

CHAPTER 6

A siren wails toward us, then another. They wake Gabi from her trance. "Change seats with me!" she whispers.

I hear her words, but they make no sense to me. "What?"

Gabi's voice is full of cold authority. "I can't be driving. Change seats and tell the cops you were at the wheel."

This is another side of Gabi I've never seen. I hesitate. She is not asking me to change seats so she can have a better view at the movies. She's asking me to lie.

"It's your fault!" Gabi says. "You brought the booze! You made me drink it."

That's not what I remember. But I don't have the strength to argue. Gabi must sense this, because she jumps out of the car and runs around to open my door. "Slide over!"

My knee hurts so much that I don't want to budge. But the sirens are getting louder and Gabi shouts like a drill sergeant, "Move!"

I have to lift my leg over the gearshift. The pain gets so bad I almost throw up. But I manage to slump into the driver's seat before two patrol cars arrive.

One car blocks the road. Another officer puts traffic cones at the other end of the street.

The cop from the second car walks toward us. His head swivels, taking in the whole scene, including Vera's body.

He pulls the radio off his belt and talks into it briefly. I hear a bunch of initials that make no sense: VCU, DWI, HCIFS.

Then I hear the static of the dispatcher's

reply. I'm not sure what will happen next. I only know that we're in trouble that's as deep as it gets.

"Thanks," Gabi murmurs.

I don't know what to say. Everything happened too fast. How did I wind up taking the blame? My knee hurts more than anything I've ever felt. My neck isn't much better. I can't think straight.

More sirens wail toward us. I'm glad to see the ambulance. I hope they give me some painkillers soon!

EMTs immediately start treating my knee. They shine lights in my eyes and ask questions like "What's your name? What year is this?"

One gives me a shot that makes the pain fade almost instantly. He's so fast with the needle I don't even notice the prick. Or maybe everything else just hurts so much more.

The cop introduces himself as Officer Sanchez. He looks a little like my soccer coach, Mr. Wunderman. I find myself wanting to like him.

He writes down our names, including

Vera's. Gabi bursts into tears. Sanchez listens as we describe the accident.

The EMTs treat the raw spots on Gabi's forearms. One reports to Sanchez, "Just the usual airbag burns, and some bruising on her left collarbone."

Sanchez looks her in the eyes and asks, "Were you driving this vehicle?"

Gabi shakes her head, hiding her face in a dark veil of silky hair.

Sanchez persists, "How did you get those scrapes on your arms?"

Gabi cries a bunch of pretty tears. Even knowing that she's in the middle of a good girl act, my heart melts a little. She looks like a fairy-tale princess in distress.

I guess the cop has seen plenty of tears in his time. He just hands Gabi a tissue and says, "I see from the registration that it's your family's car. Why was Roberto driving?"

Gabi shrugs. Her voice is small and muffled by sobs. "He . . . wanted to . . . drive."

The officer speaks a little louder, as if trying to encourage Gabi to speak up too.

Gabi dabs at her tears.

The cop turns to me and asks, "Were you holding the steering wheel when the airbag deployed?"

Through the curtain of her hair, Gabi's eyes find mine. I manage to lie, "Of course."

Sanchez sighs. "Why don't you have marks on your arms from the bag?"

Gabi looks at me and says, "We don't have to say anything without a lawyer."

The officer replies, "There'll be plenty of time to talk after your injuries have been treated." He asks the EMTs, "Will she need additional medical attention?"

After a few tests and questions, the EMTs say Gabi and Adam are fine.

Sanchez asks Gabi if she is willing to submit to a blood alcohol test. The black pits of her eyes seek mine. I shrug. What can we do? Won't they be suspicious if she refuses? Is she even allowed to refuse?

The cop sighs. "If we have to get a warrant . . ."

Gabi shakes her head. I guess she realizes

that making them get a warrant would mean practically admitting that she's drunk.

The EMTs load us both into the ambulance. The DWI Task Force officers tell us to track their moving fingers with our eyes. They ask us a few questions. So does the guy in a suit. He says he's an assistant district attorney.

There's so much to take in, so many names, all very official. They seem so cool and controlled. I wonder if they hate us for being three more stupid teenagers whose good time turned into disaster. But they don't seem angry, just detached and maybe a little sad.

Gabi just keeps crying and staring at me with those big, black eyes.

Through the closing ambulance doors I see guys taking pictures of Vera. I close my eyes but still see the same bloody view. I know I'm never going to forget it.

CHAPTER 7

On the way to the hospital, the EMTs fix me up with an IV of pain medication. It works even better than the shot. The clear liquid in the bag floats me a little further away from this whole mess. I almost feel like I could leave my body completely, like I could drift out the back of the ambulance up into the blue sky.

Gabi's sobs bring me back to reality. We're in trouble, big trouble. My leg might be totally trashed. Vera's dead!

Gabi cries like she's never going to stop. Her moans mix with the siren's wail. The sound starts to grate on me. And her face looks almost hideous, all red and soggy and contorted. I know it's terrible, but I just want to shake her until she stops. I look away so she won't see the disgust in my eyes.

We hear other sirens, and I realize we must be getting close to the hospital. Since I was born, I haven't spent much time in hospitals. I had my tonsils out when I was young, but I don't even remember it. We visited Grandpa when he was dying of lung cancer. And I came with Dad to pick up Luis the time he broke his arm. But that's been it until now.

The ambulance doors open, and one of the cops leads Gabi away by the elbow. She looks over her shoulder at me.

I sort of hate her, although I feel sorry for her too. She's so afraid! But it's the kind of fear that's dangerous. I worry that she'd do anything to protect herself—even if it means making me suffer in her place.

As they wheel my stretcher into the building, I see a big clock on the wall. I can't believe that less than an hour ago, Gabi and I were kissing on the grass together, and I was hoping she would be the one.

CHAPTER 8

I hear the cop with Gabi tell someone, "She needs the mandatory blood test for alcohol and other intoxicants."

She's gone before I can even say good-bye or good luck. Of course, no amount of luck will hide the Southern Comfort in her veins. And it certainly can't bring Vera back to life.

I'm not sure who's a nurse and who's a doctor. But someone says, "We need X-rays on this young man's knee and neck."

A nurse cuts off my jeans. Firm but gentle hands position me for the two sets of X-rays. The doctor and technician exchange a bunch of medical words that I don't understand.

A nurse adjusts a brace around my neck. "How does that feel?"

Suddenly I realize she's talking *to* me, not *about* me to another doctor.

I part my lips and manage to say, "It's okay."

Maybe the nurse can see the fear in my eyes, because she says, "The X-rays confirm that it's only whiplash. Very painful, but that will go away in time. You'll be fine after it's had a chance to heal."

I'm embarrassed because I suddenly realize I'm crying. I'm scared to death of being paralyzed.

The nurse hands me a tissue and whispers, "It's okay. Everyone gets scared. You'll be okay."

I exhale a long, uneven breath. How long had I been holding it?

The nurse says, "The doctor will tell you more about your knee soon. But you won't lose the leg or end up in a wheelchair."

More hot tears roll out of my eyes. The

nurse pats my shoulder and repeats, "It's okay. You'll be okay."

I wonder how many times a day she says that. And does she always mean it? Still, I cling to her words. "It's okay. I will be okay."

Mom gets to the hospital just before Dad. They're both frantic. I can tell Dad is angry, but he's also very tender. "*Hijo!* We could've lost you!" He hugs me so hard I wince.

The doctor tells us I'm going to need a knee replacement. Mom and Dad exchange worried looks. The doctor adds, "The recovery will be very painful. But this surgery will give Roberto the best chance of regaining full use of his leg."

Full use. That's a scary phrase. It implies that partial use is possible.

I try not to cry again, but it isn't easy. Am I going to be limping around on a cane for the rest of my life?

I swallow hard around the lump in my throat. Finally, I manage to ask the doctor, "Will I be able to play soccer?"

He replies, "It's too soon to tell."

CHAPTER 9

I want to know what's going on with Gabi. But my parents tell me to rest.

"Just get well," Dad says. His jaw clenches. "We'll talk about this more when you're feeling better."

Mom adds, "You have a big day tomorrow."

I haven't had surgery since my tonsils and I'm scared. I'm not even sure what a knee replacement is, and I'm feeling too embarrassed to ask questions. Will they be putting in some piece of metal where my knee used to be?

If it's like an organ transplant, can my body reject it? Or will it be sort of cool? I saw a TV show one time where a soldier who got his legs blown off by a bomb got these new metal legs that made it possible for him to run even faster than someone with real legs. Still, I bet he wishes he still had his own legs. Maybe I'll have tough-looking scars.

"This might be a good time to pray," Mom says. She folds her hands and looks at me.

Dad shrugs. "It couldn't hurt to check in with the man upstairs." I see another flash of anger in his eyes before he looks down at his hands.

I think of Gabi's plaid skirt and the rest of her phony good girl act. Is she praying in front of the cops? Is she asking for forgiveness? Or is she still trying to blame me for everything?

I want to pray and feel at peace, the way I did when I was really little and Mom would take us to confession. But I can't seem to turn off my brain enough to focus.

The cop saw the marks on Gabi's arms and the bruise from the driver's side safety belt.

They must know she was driving. Are they grilling her in jail? Will she clam up until her parents get her a lawyer?

All that corny stuff I was feeling when we were rolling around on the grass seems so stupid now. I'd actually pictured Gabi in a wedding dress. She would look so beautiful! It'd be that whole princess thing, only real.

I figured we'd be smart and wait until after she graduated from med school. And I'd be a soccer star, or at least a college graduate, maybe coaching soccer somewhere like Mr. Wunderman.

I even pictured us having kids.

I try to remember what made me think she was so great. Not just her hair, eyes, lips, and legs. Wasn't there something more?

I remember our first kiss. It had been like Christmas morning when you're a little kid. I had felt that same tingle of joy and anticipation.

Now that sweet memory is all jumbled up with Gabi screaming at me to take her place in the driver's seat.

I also keep seeing her tossing back that Southern Comfort, saying, "I've been sneaking out of my house since I was fourteen."

Mom concludes her silent prayer with a whispered, "Amen."

Dad mumbles an "Amen" too.

I don't know if he was really praying or just playing along for Mom's sake. He once told me he'd rather watch football on Sundays than attend Mass. But he goes to church now and then for Mom's sake. "It makes her happy," he says.

I wonder what it's like to love someone enough that you're happy because they're happy. I thought I was going to feel that for Gabi. Now I don't even know who she is.

Mom sighs and stands up. She says to me, "I need to get home and take care of your brothers and sisters."

Luis, Lucinda, Ramon, and Raquel seem a million miles away. I shudder. What will they think of their big brother now? Will they still look up to me if I become a cripple?

Mom adds, "Will you two be all right here?"

I want to nod, but the brace stops me. I mumble, "Yeah. We're fine."

Dad stands up to kiss her good-bye. She hugs him hard and says something I can't hear. Then, in a louder voice, she says, "I'll keep your dinner warm."

Dad kisses her again. "I'll stay till the nurses kick me out. I'll call you before I leave."

Mom kisses my forehead. "I didn't hear an Amen from you."

I shrug and it makes my neck ache. Then I fold my hands again. This time I manage to muster something like a prayer. "Please, God, help me get through this. Please forgive me for . . ."

The prayer stalls out at the image of Vera's brains on the pavement. Then I see Gabi's mouth shouting, "Move!"

I clench my fists and try to get my thoughts under control. The best I can do is mutter "Amen," so Mom won't worry too much. I figure I can straighten things out with God later, if there is a God.

Dad looks up from his hands to my face. I see that flash of anger again. He's always been a little scary. Sometimes a lot scary. I guess fathers are supposed to be. I want to look away, but the brace prevents me from turning my head. And his angry eyes have clamped on mine.

"So—is there anything you want to tell me, *hijo*?" I get the feeling he's not so much asking as telling.

An awkward silence settles between us. His breathing is heavy, like the snorting of a bull. I don't want to wave any red flags. I'd rather run out of the pasture. But my leg is busted—and so am I.

"Don't you want to tell me where the four of you got that liquor?"

He knows. He knows I took it from our house!

I don't want to cry, but the hot tears pour down my face. I blubber like a stupid kid. "I took it from the liquor cabinet."

Dad pounds his fist so hard on the bedside table that the tissue box bounces onto the floor. He hisses, "We trusted you!"

I don't know what to say. So I mutter, "I'm sorry, Dad!"

"Sorry? You're sorry? You bet you're sorry!"

His voice is so loud one of the nurses ducks

into the room. Dad sighs and tells her, "I'll try to keep my voice down."

She nods. "Please."

Then he does something even worse than yelling. Dad puts his head in his hands and moans. "*Hijo mio!* What have you done?"

Once again, I don't know what to say. This morning I would have said, "I was just trying to have a little fun." But now, with Vera dead, that excuse seems worse than lame.

When Dad picks up his head, I see tears in his eyes. Dad never cries, except at funerals.

I don't want to cry, but the tears flow anyway. Dad blows his nose. Then he takes another tissue and gently wipes my face.

"You should rest," he says. He blows his nose again before adding, "I'll yell at you when you get better."

I try to smile, but it doesn't work.

Dad pats my shoulder and repeats, "Rest now."

━━ ━━ ━━ ━━ ━━

I don't remember falling asleep. I wake up to

see Dad standing over me.

"*Hijo*," he whispers. "I'm supposed to leave now."

Dad hugs me too hard again. My eyes fill with tears. It isn't really from pain. It's more the way the hug takes me back to being his little boy. There was a time when the worst thing on my conscience was sneaking into the cookie jar or teasing Lucy until she cried.

Now one of my friends is dead, and I . . .

My thoughts start churning again. I wasn't driving. I wasn't even that drunk. It isn't all my fault, the way Gabi said it was. So why do I feel . . . ?

The nurse comes in and Dad hugs me once more. "We'll see you in the morning. *Buenas noches, mi'ijo.*"

As soon as Dad leaves, the nurse gives me a sleeping pill. I'm afraid I'll have nightmares. I don't want to see Vera's brains on the pavement anymore. I don't want to remember the sick weightless feeling as the car flipped.

But the pill works fast. Suddenly I'm nowhere. And then it's morning.

CHAPTER 10

When I wake up, I don't have much time to worry. My surgery is scheduled early. My parents barely have time to wish me luck before I'm wheeled into pre-op.

A nurse gives me a shot and tells me to start counting backward from one hundred.

— — — —

I wake up in the recovery room. I feel cold

but okay. Nurses take my pulse, and a doctor shines a light in my eyes. They speak around me again and write things on my chart.

As the fog clears, it starts to make me mad that no one's talking *to* me. I say, "Hello?"

The nurse pats my shoulder. "Hello, Roberto! You came through the surgery just fine."

"A complete success," the doctor adds. "The rest is up to you now."

I hear a familiar voice outside the door. It's Mom. "How is he? I want to see my son!"

The nurse rushes to the door. "I'm sorry, Mrs. Ramirez. Family's not allowed in the recovery room. But Roberto is fine. Really. We'll be moving him shortly. We just want to give him a little more time to recover from the anesthesia."

Mom looks past the nurse's shoulder to wave at me. Her smile is huge. Her eyes are bright with tears.

I try to lift my arm to wave. But it feels like it weighs a ton! Trying to do anything makes me dizzy. So I just smile back at her.

Dad waves over Mom's head. "We'll see you soon," he says, then puts his arm around Mom's shoulder and leads her away.

I sag back onto the pillow, close my eyes, and wait for my head to stop spinning.

The next time I wake up I feel much better. I can move my arms. But when I try to wiggle my feet, pain surges up from my bandaged knee.

The doctor tells me, "The good news is, you'll only need to stay in the hospital for a couple of days. The bad news is that your recovery is going to hurt. A lot. Painful as it is, we're going to get you back on your feet right away. You'll have physical therapy several times a day. And even after you go home, you must do all the exercises every day. Do you understand?"

I try to nod, but the brace stops me. So I promise, "I will!"

I want to walk, to run, and to play soccer again. I'm used to exercising. It'll be like drills with the team, I think.

Soon I'm in a room with Mr. Kravitz. He's

an old man recovering from a broken hip. He says the cast is driving him crazy. "Everything itches!" He complains about the nurses, the doctors, the food, and the TV. Then he apologizes for complaining.

I try to tune him out, but the only things competing for my attention are the tremendous pain in my leg and the lingering ache in my neck.

Even with all the painkillers, my knee hurts more than I thought anything could hurt.

I want to be brave. I tell myself it could be worse. I could have lost a leg! Or I could be dead like Vera.

I want to be brave. But mostly I just clench my teeth and moan.

CHAPTER 11

Adam stops by to see me. There's so much I want to say to him. But my throat is tight with tears. I only manage to croak out a few words: "I'm so sorry about Vera!"

Adam nods. I know how he feels. If he speaks, he'll cry. And who wants to do any more crying?

I know I should ask about Vera's mom. But I already know the answer. She must be a mess! Vera's dad left when she was very young.

Vera was her mom's whole world.

Adam's eyes meet mine for a few seconds before he looks away. We've hung out together for so many years. But this is the biggest thing either one of us has ever had to deal with. We don't know what to say.

After an awkward silence, we both start talking at once. Usually that's enough to crack us up. Now it just sends us back into silence.

Finally, I take a deep breath and start again. "I'm so sorry! I shouldn't have brought that liquor."

Adam's eyes meet mine again. They look like deep, empty pits.

I know what he's thinking. He was the one who suggested alcohol in the first place. But I can't stand to see him so sad. And besides, he isn't the only one to blame. Vera teased Gabi until she drank. Vera took off her seat belt. Gabi drove drunk.

We're all in this mess together. I want to ask Adam, how do we get out? When do things start to get better?

Adam sighs. I guess he doesn't know either.

I make a feeble joke. "So, I'm part robot now."

Adam tries to smile, but his lips quit halfway through.

"Hurts like hell," I add.

Adam looks down at the floor and says something strange: "I envy you."

I'm not sure I heard him right. "What?"

Adam keeps his eyes on his sneakers as he explains. "Wish I hurt on the outside, instead of just on the inside."

I try to lighten the mood again. "Yeah, well, I know it's the only thing that's kept my old man from tearing me to pieces."

Adam attempts to smile again. His eyes don't play along.

I want to say something wise and comforting like a friend would on TV or in movies. I want to assure Adam that "we'll get through this together" or "Vera's in a better place now." But I don't know how to even start.

The silence between us hurts almost as much as my knee. So I keep trying to fill it. I ask, "So how's school?"

Adam shakes his head. "Haven't been back yet."

"When . . . ?" I don't even finish the question.

He shrugs. "Not sure. Can't . . ." His voice trails off.

"I talked to my brothers and sisters on the phone earlier. Luis told me everyone is talking about the accident, even in middle school."

Adam shrugs.

News travels fast at Southside High. And news this big was probably all over the TV and the local paper.

I couldn't go to Vera's funeral. But I saw pictures from it on the news. I tell Adam, "I wish I could have gone to the service."

Adam shakes his head. "No, you don't." His voice is husky with tears when he explains, "Vera's mom almost fainted. Vera's uncle had to hold her up. Her grandmother just kept staring at me. Every time I looked up, there she was!"

"It's not your fault," I say.

Adam looks through me with his strange, dark eyes.

"It's my fault," I add. "And Gabi's too."

Adam mumbles, "Whatever."

The last time a student died, our principal held an assembly. A counselor, Mrs. Renner, spoke and invited everyone to come see her. I'm thinking maybe Adam ought to make a visit.

"Have you . . . been to the counselor?" I ask.

Adam groans. "Stages of grief, blah, blah, blah."

I want to ask him if the other kids know I wasn't driving. But it seems selfish. Vera is dead. Does it really matter who was behind the wheel? We all shared in the mistake. I just wish I had a time machine or something. I wish I could go back and do things right.

As we start to fall into another silence, Adam slowly lifts a hand. He waves and mutters, "See you."

When he's in the doorway, Adam looks over his shoulder and says, "Feel better soon."

"You too," I reply.

But I know that neither one of us will for a long time. I'm almost jealous of Vera. Her problems are over.

I know it's wrong to even think like that. Who knows? Maybe dead people have problems too. Or maybe they're just gone. And the people who loved them are left with holes in their lives.

I don't want to think about Vera's mom, or her grandmother, or all the students and teachers from Southside who crowded into the funeral home. I don't want to think about how many of them probably blame me for what happened. But my brain won't shut up!

I get so mad I throw a plastic cup across the room. It isn't as satisfying as I'd hoped— the cup just taps against the wall and falls to the floor.

Mr. Kravitz looks up from the cup to me. I blush and say, "Sorry."

His eyes meet mine and he says, "It's all right. Being in pain'll make you mad, all right."

I don't mind his complaining so much after that. A broken hip probably hurts more than a busted knee.

CHAPTER 12

As soon as I can, I call Gabi. Her voice sounds low and muffled, like she's far away.

"It's me," I say, in case she didn't recognize my hello.

She doesn't answer. So I ask, "How are you?"

I hear her sigh. Then there's a silence just as awkward as the one with Adam.

"Where are you?" I ask.

"At home," Gabi replies. "I only spent a

few hours in jail before my parents paid bail. They got a lawyer too."

I figure her folks must be furious! My parents haven't mentioned the doctor bills. But this accident will probably bust their budget, even with insurance. When I get well, I'm going to have to find a way to make it up to them. I'll probably have to get a summer job. Or two.

Gabi starts to sob. "I've been charged with Intoxicated Manslaughter. Charged as an adult. It's a second-degree felony. Do you know what that means? I'll be a criminal. It'll go on my permanent record."

My mind reels. She won't be able to vote. She won't be able to get a good job. And her chance of a scholarship to a fancy medical school is probably long gone.

"I could go to jail for twenty years!" Gabi wails.

I can't believe it. "You won't! It was an accident."

Gabi sighs. "It doesn't matter—my life is ruined!"

I know I should say something to comfort her. But my knee throbs. And a nasty part of me thinks, "And you tried to ruin mine!"

Sure I brought the booze. But she didn't have to drink so much of it! She didn't have to swerve for some stupid armadillo.

Gabi's voice is flat with despair. "I shouldn't have drunk. I shouldn't have drunk."

I can't argue with that. Her voice dissolves into sobs. Even over the phone I can tell these aren't "pretty tears." This is anguish.

I suddenly panic, picturing Gabi as dead as Vera. "Look—don't do anything stupid, Gabi!"

Gabi sniffles. "Too late."

"I mean . . ." I don't even want to say it. "Don't hurt yourself."

Gabi sighs. "Whatever."

"Promise me!" I shout, sounding like Dad. I'm angry at her too. But I don't want Gabi to die. "Dying won't bring back Vera. It would only make things worse."

Gabi doesn't answer, just breathes raggedly.

"Promise me!" I repeat.

Gabi sighs again. "Okay. I promise."

I wish I could believe her.

"My parents are making me go back to school tomorrow," Gabi says. She sobs again. "I don't think I can take it! Everyone's going to be looking at me . . ."

Her voice trails off. I don't know what to say to her. So I try repeating what the nurse said to me. "It'll be okay."

Gabi snaps. "Really? What makes you say that?"

"I . . . you know . . ." I fumble around, not finding an answer. Then I hear Gabi's mother in the background. "Who's that on the phone?"

"Just Nancy again. She forgot to tell me the trig assignment." Gabi lies easily. Then she whispers to me, "Please don't call me again. I'll call you when I can."

I hang up the phone and mutter to myself. "And when will that be? When you need someone to blame?"

CHAPTER 13

In between painkiller doses, there's no getting away from the pain in my knee. TV's no distraction either. Everyone's still talking about the accident. They're all saying that Vera was "so wonderful" and "full of promise."

I fumble with the remote, trying to change the channel before I hear one more person describe Vera as this beacon of light.

Vera was Vera. Why do they have to turn her into someone else? It reminds me of all those movies where the hero's perfect blonde wife gets killed at the beginning so he can go on this rampage of righteous revenge.

Nobody's perfect. Can't we be sad that Vera died just because she was Vera? Why do we have to pretend she was perfect?

I liked her laugh. I liked the way she made fun of the lunchroom lady. She always baked cupcakes for everyone's birthday. She collected snow globes from tourist shops—the cornier the better.

Vera loved buying new shoes and new clothes. She wanted to be America's Next Top Model. She probably wouldn't have made it. Vera was very pretty. But she wasn't model pretty. She was the kind of pretty that grew on you after you got to know her.

And now she's just a memory. Somehow it makes me mad that instead of remembering the real Vera, the media is turning her into some kind of saint.

Vera wasn't a saint! If she hadn't been so eager to sit on Adam's lap . . . If she'd only worn her seat belt . . .

She was just a girl with a big crush on my best friend. Vera was just Vera. I miss her. And I'm sorry for the part I played in her death.

Other people get away with doing bad things all the time. Why couldn't I skip class just once? Why couldn't Gabi drive drunk once without ruining all our lives?

I keep flipping across channels, but it's all junk. Even good shows seem stupid. And sports just make me worry about whether I'll ever play soccer again.

CHAPTER 14

I can't believe I've only been in the hospital for two days. It feels like forever.

My folks come to the hospital right at the start of visiting hours. Mom looks tired. Dad looks worried. I try to tell them, "You don't have to stay here. I'm okay."

But as soon as they leave the room, I plunge into loneliness.

Most of my soccer buddies call. They say the usual greeting card stuff. You know, "feel better soon," lots of wishes on a quick recovery.

I ask them about practice and Coach Wunderman. I want to think about something other than the accident and my knee.

My teammate Benito wonders, "Did you really make Gabi tell the cops she was driving even though you were at the wheel?"

I can hardly believe what I'm hearing. "What?"

"That's what Gabi told her friends," Benito says. "They're telling everyone else that you were driving, but you made her take the blame because you don't have a license."

I get so mad I punch the mattress. The impact makes my neck throb. That lying little . . .

Curse words flood my mind as Benito chatters on. "I told the guys you wouldn't do that. But everyone knows you don't have your license and Gabi . . ."

I get it. Gabi's pretty. I'm just a guy stupid enough to fall for her act.

"She was driving," I say flatly. "Ask the

cops. Why do you think *she* was arrested?"

"That's what I said!" Beni exclaims. "But Gabi said they were taking it easy on you because of your knee."

I keep myself from punching the mattress again. But God do I want to.

"Can she explain why it's my left knee that was messed up by the gearshift and not my right?"

Beni chuckles. "I told everyone that girl was lying. But you know how people are. They believe whoever's talking, especially if it's big gossip like that."

My heart sinks. I've known kids whose reputations were ruined by one mistake. Sexy pictures on the Internet, exes spreading nasty stories, and all that.

I always used to figure, "Who cares what everybody thinks, as long as you know who you are? But the thought that everyone's blaming me for killing Vera, and that Gabi is deliberately spreading that lie, makes me want to puke!

"Coach says he can't wait for you to come back," Benito says.

I'm not sure I ever want to go back to Southside. But what choice do I have? I'm not a quitter. I tell Beni, "I'll be back as soon as I get off the walker and onto a cane. It could be a couple of weeks."

"Does it hurt a lot?"

"Yeah." It hurts almost as much as being betrayed by the girl you thought you loved.

I hear a knock and look up to see Father Mike standing in the doorway.

I tell Benito, "Looks like I have a visitor."

"That's cool," Beni says. "I better get my homework done anyway. Take care, Rob!"

Before I say good-bye, I add, "Thanks for calling. And for sticking up for me!"

"No problem."

As I hang up the phone, the priest walks into the room. "Sorry to interrupt your call. I was visiting another parishioner and heard you were here, so I thought I'd stop by. Is this a good time?"

Normally I like seeing Father Mike's round, kindly face. But now I just want to run away from him. If only I could run.

Father Mike pats my shoulder. "It's natural to feel angry when bad things happen." Can he read my mind—or just my scowl? "Peace will come in time," he adds.

I don't believe him. I think Gabi was right about one thing. Our lives are ruined! And what can we do?

"How are you feeling?" Father Mike says.

I glance over at Mr. Kravitz, then say, "I hate to complain, but my knee hurts, my neck hurts, and I just found out the chick I thought was my girlfriend is telling everyone at Southside I'm the one who was driving the car."

Father Mike gives a low whistle. "I'm sorry to hear that, Roberto. Is there anything I can do to help?"

My fists clench with frustration. I want to say, "You could leave before you start spouting any useless words of comfort." But I have enough on my conscience without insulting a priest.

"Would it help to know that God knows the truth?" His warm brown eyes seek mine.

I look away before he can see what I'm thinking. No, it doesn't really help, because then God knows that I snuck out that bottle of Southern Comfort. He saw me rolling on the grass with Gabi. He must've seen the armadillo. Couldn't God have pushed it aside? Or made Gabi a better driver?

I sigh.

Father Mike pats my shoulder. "Sometimes even good people make bad choices. Try to forgive the others—and yourself. Have faith."

I'm not sure I believe in faith anymore. Luckily, a nurse comes in to poke and prod me, so I don't have to listen to any more well-intentioned preaching.

CHAPTER 15

I can't believe how much it hurts to walk on my new knee. I lean on the walker like an old man. Pain shoots up my leg anyway. My eyes water. Every step feels like I'm being stabbed.

Ed, the physical therapist, stays at my side. I want to stop, but Ed keeps telling me, "Just a little more. That's good!"

Ed's a young guy with big muscles. He looks like he belongs in a weight room or on a football field, not in a hospital.

"You don't look like the medical type," I say.

Ed chuckles. "You mean my muscles are showing through my scrubs?"

"Yeah, most of the doctors . . ." my voice trails off. My knee hurts so much I'm having trouble finding words.

Ed flashes an easy smile. "Most of the doctors don't look like such jocks."

I can't help smiling, even though my knee is killing me. "Yeah," I gasp. "Exactly."

We've reached the end of the hall. That's a big victory! Only two more laps before I get to rest for a while.

Ed helps me turn around with the walker. "I was a football player," he explains. "Had a scholarship, plans to go pro. Then a busted ankle put me on the sidelines for a whole season."

"And you decided to quit?" I ask.

Ed shakes his head. "I decided to do something different with my life. I could've gone back to football. Maybe my ankle would've been okay. Maybe not. Maybe I could've gone all the way to the Super Bowl. Who knows? But to tell you the truth, I like this better. I still play most weekends, but touch, not tackle. We don't have to play if the weather's bad or if we don't feel like it. We play for fun. And every workday, I get to help people like you."

I've been so busy listening, I actually almost forget about my knee for a few seconds. It gives me hope that eventually I'll be able to walk without pain. Won't that be amazing? You never realize how precious some things are until you lose them.

We've reached the other end of the hall. Ed raises his arms like an Olympic athlete winning the gold. "You made it! Just one more lap before you nap."

I manage a wobbly smile and a sarcastic "Whoopee!" Then Ed helps me make the turn. The end of the hall looks so far away. But I'm determined to get there.

Ed gives me a double thumbs-up and another one of his big smiles. "You can do it, Roberto!"

With his bulging arms and chest straining at the crisp fabric of his scrubs, it's easy to

picture him in a football uniform. I always
thought medicine was for good girls like Gabi
or guys with thick glasses. I never realized
a jock could also wear scrubs. But Ed seems
happy. On the last lap, he even confides that
he makes "a decent living."

CHAPTER 16

Benito calls me again the next day. "I told the team what you told me about Gabi lying and your left knee and all," he says. "They said they'd try to spread your side of the story."

"Thanks!" I reply.

It feels odd to have someone other than Adam acting like my best friend. But I guess Adam's too freaked out to be anyone's friend right now.

Of course, when I think back on all the years of our friendship, I have to admit we spent most of our time just goofing around. Was he ever truly my friend or just someone to hang out with? There's a difference, I've decided.

"Gabi isn't returning to Southside," Beni adds. "She's back at St. Michael's. One of her friends told me there's not even going to be a trial."

"What does that mean?"

"She's pleading guilty. And because she's a good girl with no previous record, she probably won't have to spend too many years in prison."

I wonder how many pretty tears that will take. But I guess it doesn't really matter. Prison won't bring Vera back to life.

Beni tries to cheer me up. "At least you won't have to testify."

That's true. I won't have to get up in front of a bunch of strangers and admit I sneaked that bottle out of my parents' liquor cabinet. And I won't have to watch Gabi cry while she tries to blame me.

I won't ever have to see her beautiful face again. And that is a relief.

"Do you want me to get your assignments for you?" Beni asks. "The teachers won't want you to fall too far behind."

Schoolwork will seem like a treat after what I've been through. I tell Benito, "Yeah, thanks. That'd be great."

"I can get your schedule from Luis on the bus tomorrow morning and give him your assignments on the way home," he says.

"I'll give you my locker combination, if you don't mind carrying my books."

"What are friends for?"

I think about all the times Adam has gotten me in trouble, leading up to now. The only time I ever shoplifted, Adam dared me into it. I was the one who got caught and grounded for a month.

One day we peeked into the girls' locker room. That was Adam's idea. We didn't get caught, but Luis found out and told Mom and Dad. I got grounded for two months.

Was there ever a time Adam got grounded

because of me? I can't remember any. Adam's mom doesn't bother punishing him. She can never make a punishment stick, anyway.

I realize there are good friends and bad friends. And there are surprising friends, like Benito. I've always liked playing soccer with him. But we've never hung out much. And now that I'm in trouble, here he is. How cool is that?

"Well, I'll call again later, Rob," Beni says. "Hang in there!"

Before he ends the call, I say, "Yeah, thanks a lot!"

CHAPTER 17

M y folks have set me up on the couch in the den since I can't walk upstairs yet.

It feels great to be home and to see my brothers and sisters. I didn't even realize how much I missed the four pests until their faces greet me at the door.

Luis teases me. "Don't cry, Berto!" But I can tell he's glad to see me too. Lucy, Ramon, and Raquel all make a big fuss.

I can't believe how happy I am just to be

sitting at the dinner table with my family again. Mom cooks all my favorite foods because "this is a celebration!" Lucy and Raquel keep hopping up to get me things.

After dinner, I hobble back to the couch. I'm too tired to face the homework Luis brought from Beni. I figure it can wait until tomorrow.

While everyone else watches TV, Dad tucks me in. His face looks grim. He promised to yell at me when I was well. I'm not exactly well yet. But I brace myself for a lecture.

Dad sighs. "I did not want to spoil your mother's nice dinner. But you know we aren't done with this."

I nod. "What I did was wrong. And I wish I could go back and change it."

Dad flinches at the word *wish*. He says, "Wishes are for fools and children. I thought you were on your way to being a man."

"I just meant . . ."

Dad's fierce glare stops me mid-excuse. There is no excuse.

"Roberto, I hardly know where to begin. You took something that didn't belong to you, something you clearly are not mature enough to handle. And you risked your life getting in that car with a drunk driver!"

I don't even try to defend myself. What can I say?

Dad goes on. "Your mother and I have tried to think of a punishment."

I jump in. "I'm going to pay for the operation. Every cent, if it takes me twenty years!"

Dad gives me a weary smile. "We'll see how much the insurance covers."

"I'll get two jobs!" I add.

Dad pats my shoulder. "First, you have to get well and . . . you'll have to find jobs close to home or the bus lines. Because your mother and I have decided that we are not going to let you retake your driver's exam for a year."

I might as well be grounded! Every other senior either already has a driver's license or will have one soon. It'll just be me and the legally blind guy begging rides from everyone else.

I want to say, "No!" But one look at Dad's face and I know this is well past the discussion stage. My folks aren't like Adam's mom. When they decide on a punishment, they stick to it. If you try to get out of it, they just make it worse. And I don't want to wait *two* years for my license. So I keep my mouth shut.

Dad lets the reality of my sentence sink in before he adds, "Roberto, you have to start thinking things through like a grown man. You can't just wish for things to go your way. You can't trust luck.

"You might have been lucky. You might have gotten away with stealing that liquor. Gabi might have gotten away with driving drunk. But you didn't. Some chances aren't worth taking."

Tears fill my eyes. I'm thinking of Vera. We all took a chance, and she lost everything.

Dad pats my good leg. "Remember how Grandpa used to bet on the ponies? Sometimes he'd win. Sometimes he'd lose."

I remember. Once he bought us all roller skates with his winnings. Luis broke his arm the first time we put them on! I teased him for crying. Now I understand. I bet it hurt almost as much as my knee.

Dad smiles as he remembers his father. "He always told me, 'Never make a bet you can't afford to lose.' Do you understand? Driving drunk is a bet you can't afford to lose."

Then he says to me, "Like having sex with a girl you wouldn't want to marry."

I blush. I'm not ready to get married. And I figure I'm lucky things didn't go further with Gabrielle. Sure she's beautiful. But beauty fades. Sneaky is forever.

CHAPTER 18

I'm fast asleep when Luis wakes me. It feels like the middle of the night but it's not even 8:30! He says, "Hey, Sleeping Beauty! There's a phone call for you," and hands me the phone.

"Who is it?" I ask.

He bats his eyelashes and teases, "Some girl. She didn't say."

I've been getting lots of calls since the accident. Some kids I barely know are calling, some to be nice, some because they want gossip.

I put my chin up to the receiver. "Hello?"

A muffled voice says, "It's me."

Me? Who's "me?" I wonder. It takes me a second to realize it's Gabi!

For a moment I remember feeling crazy about her, thinking that she would be my first, maybe even "the one." Now I wish we had never met. But as Dad likes to say, "Wish in one hand, spit in the other. See which fills up first."

"I feel so alone," Gabi whispers. I know what she means. "My sisters seem almost happy that 'Mommy's good girl' has fallen out of favor. My friends make a show of caring about me, but mostly they just want to hear the gory details. And I just can't—I can't talk about it. I want to run away! I can't stand it at home. It's like my parents hate me. I know they're trying to help. But they're so angry. And the lawyer is costing so much. I feel like everyone would be better off if I was just gone."

I don't like the sound of that. "Remember what you promised!" I say. "Just hang in there."

The words sound so feeble. But they are all I have to offer. And if her parents have their way, these may be our last words together.

"I wish none of this had ever happened!" Gabi says.

"Me too!"

It feels strange to be talking to her like we're friends again. Because ever since Beni told me what she was saying, I've hated Gabi. And now . . .

As if she can read my mind, Gabi says, "I don't want you to hate me too."

"I don't hate you," I say. Is that true? "I don't think your family hates you, either. They're just angry, disappointed, and all that."

Gabi sobs. "I don't know what to do!"

I think of her swerving to avoid the armadillo, then swerving sharply to get back onto the road. "Slow down! You don't have to do anything right now. Just . . . hang in there."

I know it's a stupid phrase. But what else can I say?

Mom walks into the den. "Are you still on the phone? You should get back to sleep. You need your rest. Tell your friend you can call her back in the morning."

I tell Gabi, "I have to go."

"I heard. Parents are such a pain." Her voice almost sounds normal.

"Well . . . take care," I say.

"You too." Just before she hangs up, Gabi adds, "I love you."

Mom hangs up the phone for me. Then she asks, "Who was that?"

"Just a girl from my trig class." That's not exactly a lie, because Gabi is in my math class. Although it's certainly not the whole truth like they make you tell in court. But I know if I said "Gabi," that would lead to a bunch of questions I don't feel like answering right now. My head is already swarming with my own questions.

Like, why did she say, "I love you?" She loves me? All of a sudden? Or is she trying to use me? Why?

Mom kisses my forehead and says, "You look exhausted."

I sink into the pillow and yawn. "Yeah, I guess I am."

"If anyone else calls, we'll just take a message."

My eyelids are already drooping shut as I murmur, "Thanks, Mom."

CHAPTER 19

In the middle of the night, I hear something outside. At first I think that hail is coming down. Then I realize that someone's throwing pebbles at the den window!

I hobble over to it and peer outside. A dark figure crouches in the moonlight under the window. I almost scream when the person stands up, until I see Gabi's pale face!

I flip the lock and slide the window open. Gabi smiles. "I figured you'd be in one of the downstairs rooms."

"What are you doing?" I ask.

"I'm running away. And I want you to come with me."

I hate myself for thinking this, but she looks beautiful in the moonlight. Her black hair shines like a rippling pond. Her skin looks as smooth as a Barbie doll's.

"Let me in," she whispers.

Leaning on my walker, I hobble over to the door and slowly undo the locks. *Clunk. Clunk.* They sound so loud!

I hold my breath, hoping nobody wakes up. I wait for a few seconds, listening, before I open the door.

Gabi rushes into my arms, almost knocking the walker over. She snuggles against my chest. I had forgotten how good she smells.

"I've missed you!" she whispers into my shoulder.

Her hair smells like sweet shampoo. Her heart pounds against mine like a fluttery little bird. But this . . . this is crazy!

"You can't run away!" I say.

Gabi looks up at me. Her big beautiful eyes gaze deeply into mine. "I've thought it through. I can get a job somewhere, change my name. I took all my money out of the bank. I bet it's enough to get a small apartment somewhere. Maybe I'll bleach my hair—I've always wanted to see what I'd look like as a blonde. I can just get on a bus to anywhere and disappear!"

I know she's feeling bad, probably hurting inside even worse than my knee. Still, I can't believe she's being so stupid and selfish!

"If you run, your parents will have to pay the full bail, not just the 10 percent down. They'd probably lose their house! If you think they're mad now . . ."

Gabi stomps her foot and pouts. "If you really loved me, you'd take me away from all this. I wish . . ."

I hold her chin so she has to look into my eyes. "Wish in one hand and spit in the other. See which fills up first."

Gabi frowns. "That's disgusting!"

I chuckle. "It's just an expression . . ." How can I explain it to her? "It means that wishes aren't real. Spit is real. Disgusting things are real. Like Vera being dead. And you, Adam, and I all share the blame for that."

Gabi's face hardens. This isn't what she wanted to hear. But I don't care. I go on. "You can blame me all you want," I say. "But you can't run away from the truth."

Gabi snuggles against my chest again. She whispers in this hot, husky voice, "You can have me now."

Suddenly it's like we're back rolling on the grass, like the accident never happened. I don't know which I want to do more: push her away or pull her closer!

I can't really do anything, except lean on my walker. "I can't run anywhere," I remind her. "I can't even walk with a cane yet."

Gabi sniffles. "Yeah, but . . ." She sighs. "Yeah. I guess it wasn't the smartest plan."

I want to laugh and cry at the same time. Instead, I just offer to call her a cab.

Gabi shakes her head. "No, that'd make too much noise. Besides, I need the walk. I've hardly been out of the house since . . ."

I don't make her finish the sentence. I know what she means.

Gabi hesitates in the doorway. "Good-bye, Roberto." I know she doesn't mean just tonight. She means forever.

"Good-bye, Gabrielle."

CHAPTER 20

T he next day, Adam stops by. He's not as much of a zombie as he was at the hospital. But he isn't all there, either.

I ask if he's gone back to school yet. He shakes his head. "What for?"

"Adam, you have to finish. You can't drop out."

He shrugs.

I hate to see him so lost. I'm almost afraid to mention her name. So I whisper, "Vera wouldn't want you to give up on your life."

Adam changes the subject. He asks me about the surgery and my scholarship. I tell him my knee will probably be fine once I finish the physical therapy.

His lips almost manage a full smile, but there are dark circles around his eyes. He mumbles, "Nothing's ever going to be the same."

I look him right in the eyes and agree. "No, it won't."

I know that I will never take life for granted again. I won't assume everything will be okay. Because I know for a fact that sometimes it isn't.

Adam shakes his head. "I keep seeing Vera in my dreams."

"Is she . . ." I see the bloody body on the ground.

Adam shakes his head again. "She's fine. She's just . . . there. And I even tell her, 'You're dead.' But she doesn't seem to understand."

I shrug. My neck only hurts a little. "Maybe she just misses you or something." It's a dumb thing to say. I don't really believe in ghosts.

Adam smirks, and I see a hint of his old sly smile. "Maybe I'm just going crazy."

I try to get him to really smile by teasing, "*Going* crazy? You already were!"

Adam makes a feeble attempt at laughter. Then he stands up. "I've got to go."

I have the feeling he just doesn't want to stay any longer. Being around me reminds him too much of that awful day.

At the door, Adam turns and says, "See you around."

I understand what he means. We'll see each other at school, but our friendship is over. Like Vera, I guess it just couldn't survive the crash.

━━ ━━ ━━ ━━ ━━

On my first day back at Southside, Benito and the rest of the soccer team give me a big greeting. Between classes, the guys take turns carrying my books and making sure no one bumps into my cane.

By now just about everyone at school knows that I wasn't driving the day Vera died.

Some kids still blame me for bringing the booze. But that's okay. So do I. It was a dumb risk to take—the kind of bet no one can afford to lose.

I wish things had turned out differently. But I know all about wishes. They aren't worth spit.

— — — — —

After a few months, my knee is as good as new. But I'm not sure I want to be a pro soccer player anymore. I'm going to use my soccer scholarship to study physical therapy. I think Ed was right. Scoring goals is okay. But helping people every day—that's a real way to win.

About the Author

Justine Fontes and her husband, Ron, hope to write 1,001 terrific tales. So far, they have penned more than 700 children's books. They live in a quiet corner of Maine with three happy cats.

Elvis Presley

SADDLEBACK
EDUCATIONAL PUBLISHING

Saddleback's Graphic Biographies

SADDLEBACK
EDUCATIONAL PUBLISHING
Three Watson
Irvine, CA 92618-2767
Website: www.sdlback.com

ISBN-13: 978-1-59905-221-2
ISBN-10: 1-59905-221-0
eBook: 978-1-60291-584-8

Printed in China

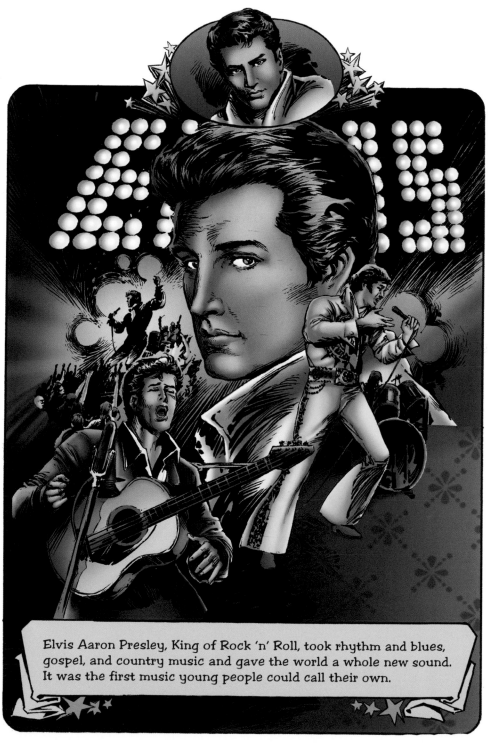

Elvis Aaron Presley, King of Rock 'n' Roll, took rhythm and blues, gospel, and country music and gave the world a whole new sound. It was the first music young people could call their own.

2

Elvis Presley was born January 8, 1935, in Tupelo, Mississippi. His parents, Vernon and Gladys Presley, lived in a two room house.

Vernon Presley worked whenever he could—sharecropping, driving a milk truck, or sorting lumber.

Gladys taught her son to be polite and kind. She took him everywhere she went. Vernon taught him to defend himself against bullies.

I like to see the minister shout, clap his hands, and get excited!

Here's your five dollar prize money and the rides are free!

When Elvis was ten, his school principal took him to the Mississippi-Alabama Fair and Dairy Show. Elvis won second prize for singing "Old Shep."

Elvis listened to the popular country music and the blues singers on the radio. He copied the sounds. He never did learn to read music, but he had a good ear for it.

Please sir, I'd like a bike.

I'm sorry son. It costs too much.

We can get you the guitar. It will help you with your singing.

First they lived in a one room apartment. Later they moved to a two bedroom apartment in a low cost housing development.

Well, there's no work here. Let's hope Memphis, Tennessee, will be better.

Vernon got a job packing paint cans starting at 83 cents an hour. Gladys sometimes worked in a curtain factory.

The high school Elvis attended had 1,600 students, more than the whole population of East Tupelo. He made some good friends. He liked football, ROTC, and shop.

Elvis sure loves football. He's good too!

The boys make fun of your hair and loud clothes, Elvis.

That doesn't bother me. They make me look older.

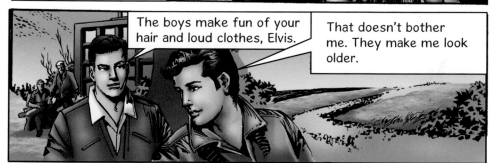

Elvis liked to sing for his friends but not in front of a group. In his senior year of high school, a teacher persuaded him to sing in the variety show. The students loved his singing.

I had to push him out for the encore. He couldn't believe he was chosen as the best of the thirty acts.

4

During high school Elvis had a few jobs. But his parents felt they interfered with his studying. Even though money was scarce, his parents always managed to give him spending money.

I like this job. I can listen to the radio. I like working, and I like to listen to music.

After high school Elvis got a job driving a truck. He made $1.25 an hour. At night he attended school to become an electrician.

You're lucky. The employment agency said you were a nice boy and not to be fooled by your long hair. The men here tease you because they like you. Remember the time they sent you to look for "sky hooks."

Then you said don't let them fool you. There is no such thing. I like them too!

Ma'am, I'd like to make a record for my mother.

In 1953 Elvis Presley paid $4 to the Memphis Recording Service to make a record for his mother. He sang "My Happiness" and a sad ballad called "That's When Your Heartache Begins."

Once that boy started to sing, I knew you should hear him, Sam. So I taped the rest.

Yes, he's different. But he needs work.

Elvis came back to make a second record.

Sam introduced Elvis to Scotty Moore, a guitar player, and Bill Black, a bass player. They worked together for months, trying to find a style of music they liked.

What the devil are you doing!

I think we have got something.

Sam took the group's first record to Dewey Phillips, a disc jockey for radio station WHBQ. Listeners began calling in asking to have the record played over and over.

I've played that record fourteen times! In a row!

Elvis turned on the radio for his parents. Then he went to a movie, too nervous to listen.

That recording by Elvis, Scotty, and Bill was historic. To "That's All Right (Mama)," the blues song, they gave a country sound.

On the other side of the single, to bluegrass hit "Blue Moon of Kentucky," Elvis sang the blues. It was the first time that country music and blues were mixed. The form later was called "rockabilly."

To perform in Nashville's Grand Ole Opry was the hope of all country and western singers. Elvis made it after his first record. But ...

Son, I suggest you go back to truck driving.

Elvis was so upset that he left a suitcase full of clothes behind.

In October 1954 the second radio booking was with the Louisiana Hayride. It was more successful.

He's great. We'll give him a year's contract.

The 3,500 seat auditorium was always filled on the Saturday nights Elvis was to appear.

TENNESSEE

MISSISSIPPI

ALABAMA

GEORGIA

FLO

TEXAS

LOUISIANA

For this I quit driving a truck—to sleep in a car?

Well, you and Bill don't own cars. Let's just hope this doesn't wear out before my wife finishes paying for it.

The group was now known as the Blue Moon Boys. Bob Neal, their manager, would book three or four shows a week at schoolhouses in the South.

Elvis was on his way up. *Billboard,* a record magazine, took notice of him.

His singing style and famous body movements were getting him a larger and larger following.

The Colonel

In 1955 Colonel Tom Parker was something of a legend. Maybe Elvis Presley would not have become a legend if it hadn't been for this showman.

Tom Parker was born in 1910 of carnival folks.

How's business, Tom?

Full house, I'm doing fine!

At seventeen, he had his own pony and monkey act.

Later he traveled with other carnivals and shows doing all kinds of work.

Here you are folks. Beautiful canaries!

He became a super salesman but sometimes not an honest one. Once he painted sparrows yellow and sold them as canaries. He cut hot dogs in half put each half at the end of the bun and relish in the middle. Then he sold them as "foot long hot dogs."

He became a press agent for carnivals, circuses, and showboats. Later he became manger for country singers Eddy Arnold and Hank Snow. He put together country shows with singers, musicians, and comedians.

O.K. Plug in the hot plate.

Colonel Parker always had chickens in a cage as a "livestock exhibit" so he wouldn't have to pay a tax for his show.

Once, when Eddy Arnold couldn't sing, the colonel brought out his "dancing chickens." He had put a hot plate under the straw, and the poor chickens stepped lively when the electricity was put on.

By late 1955 Elvis, with his hit records and appearances, was making $2,000 a week. He bought a pink Cadillac and a $40,000 Memphis home for his parents.

That boy interests me. I'll help you with his bookings.

Colonel Parker met Elvis when he appeared on the *Hank Snow Jamboree*. Hank Snow was the leading country singer and was handled by the Colonel.

With your help, I can be of assistance to your son.

In order to become Elvis' personal manager, the Colonel became friends with Vernon and Gladys Presley.

In November 1955 Elvis' manager, Bob Neal, agreed to let the Colonel take over Elvis' career.

1956 became the Year of Elvis Presley. Under the Colonel's guidance, his career skyrocketed. He appeared on TV.

He received $1,250 for the *Dorsey Brothers Stage Show*. He did five more with them. TV audiences had never seen anything like Elvis before.

You gotta stay put or you'll be out of the camera range.

He appeared twice with Milton Berle and got $5,000 for each show.

During the summer he appeared on the *Steve Allen Show* for $7,500. He wore a tuxedo and stood still for his song. The fans were upset.

And he received $50,000 for three appearances on the *Ed Sullivan Show*, the leading TV show at the time. But because of the uproar his wild movements had caused, Elvis was shown on the TV screen only from the waist up.

The Colonel made a deal with RCA Records. They bought Sam Phillips' contract for $35,000—giving a $5,000 bonus to Elvis.

Beginning with "Heartbreak Hotel," one after another of Elvis' records became number one on the charts and were million record sellers.

1956
HOUND DOG
DON'T BE CRUEL
TUTTI FRUTTI
MONEY HONEY

SHAKE, RATTLE, AND ROLL,
LOVE ME TENDER
BLUE SUEDE SHOE

1957
ALL SHOOK UP
TEDDY BEAR
LOVING YOU
JAILHOUSE ROCK

Popular music was never the same again. In the 1950s, Elvis earned more gold records than other stars did in their entire careers.

Colonel Parker made a deal with Twentieth Century Fox for Elvis to make three movies for $450,000.

Elvis' first movie, *Love Me Tender*, received poor reviews from the critics, but made Hollywood money history. The costs of making the movie were recovered in only three days after its release.

The next two pictures were also box office hits. His fans were multiplying by the thousands.

After finishing the movie, *Love Me Tender* in 1956, the Colonel booked Elvis for a cross-country singing tour. He hit the big cities this time—and made as much as $25,000 a night. In 1957 when not making movies, he also toured the country singing.

He still gets stage fright before every performance.

But as soon as he starts singing he's at ease. He creates a kind of magic both for the fans and me.

Everywhere he went he was met by screaming crowds, mostly teenage girls.

One thing Elvis learned from his mother was to always be polite and kind!

And generous! He's giving his check for this show back to Tupelo.

Ten years after winning second prize for singing "Old Shep" at the Mississippi-Alabama Fair and Dairy Show, Elvis returned.

Here you are, ladies and gentlemen. Get your picture of Elvis. Only 50 cents.

Not only did the Colonel sell pictures of Elvis at the concerts, he started an Elvis Presley industry. Every item sold brought in more money for Elvis and the Colonel. There were T-shirts, sneakers, and other types of clothing, charm bracelets, stuffed hound dogs, teddy bears, lipsticks, paper dolls, and coloring books. Plus pictures, posters, and buttons. New items appeared all the time.

In 1956 Elvis probably made as much as ten million dollars. And 1957 was a big year too!

In 1957 he bought Graceland, a thirteen acre estate just outside Memphis. It had twenty-three rooms. He had a swimming pool put in and a fun room. He also had a pool table, soda fountain, movie projector, and two televisions. He bought clothes, jewelry, and cars—Lincolns, Cadillacs, Rolls Royces, buses, trucks, and motorcycles.

You sing that church music beautifully. I've always loved it.

Elvis loved his mother and father. They lived with him at Graceland. So did his grandmother, an aunt, two uncles, and the "Memphis Mafia."

Elvis couldn't appear in public without being mobbed by teenage girls. So he had a group of close friends who were bodyguards and companions.

Why do they call you the "Memphis Mafia?"

Oh, some newspaper gave us that tag, and it stuck. We're on Elvis' payroll—take care of his bills, clothes, travel— stuff like that. And keep his fans from tearing him apart.

The only outside entertainment he had was when he rented an amusement park, roller skating rink, or movie house for the night. He and the group would invite their friends to join in the fun.

The Army

At 6:35 a.m. on March 24, 1958, Elvis, his parents, and a few friends arrived at the Memphis Local Draft Board. Elvis Presley had been drafted into the army.

Elvis may be in the army—but he won't be forgotten. His new movie *King Creole* will soon be out.

Also present were the press and the Colonel with balloons advertising Elvis' new movie, *King Creole*.

The bus taking the recruits to Fort Chaffee, Arkansas, stopped at a restaurant. Dozens of fans stormed the place, tearing Elvis' clothes.

He sat in this chair, and I waited on him.

I don't care. I grabbed it first.

Do you know how much we could get selling that hair to fans?

Hair today, gone tomorrow.

At Fort Chaffee they allowed Colonel Parker to bring in the press to follow Elvis around for several days.

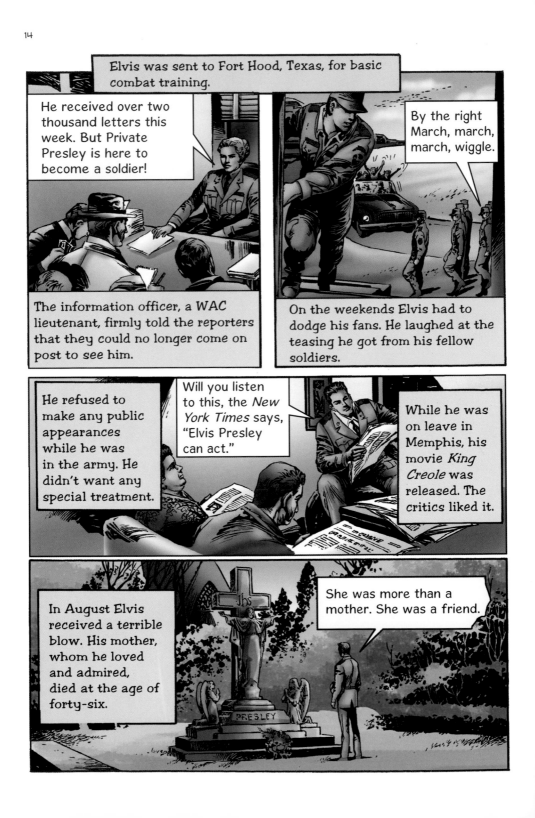

Elvis was sent to Fort Hood, Texas, for basic combat training.

He received over two thousand letters this week. But Private Presley is here to become a soldier!

The information officer, a WAC lieutenant, firmly told the reporters that they could no longer come on post to see him.

By the right March, march, march, wiggle.

On the weekends Elvis had to dodge his fans. He laughed at the teasing he got from his fellow soldiers.

He refused to make any public appearances while he was in the army. He didn't want any special treatment.

Will you listen to this, the *New York Times* says, "Elvis Presley can act."

While he was on leave in Memphis, his movie *King Creole* was released. The critics liked it.

In August Elvis received a terrible blow. His mother, whom he loved and admired, died at the age of forty-six.

She was more than a mother. She was a friend.

PRESLEY

At the end of September 1958 the army shipped Elvis to Germany. He was sent to Friedberg, near Frankfort.

Rock and roll is the biggest youth movement in Germany right now.

Hundreds of German teenage fans were kept away from Elvis.

Rent is $800 a month. You pay for repairs needed.

Stories in the papers told of his "castle." But Elvis lived off post in a plain house with his father and grandmother.

You'll need to read maps, draw sketches, and recognize the enemy.

Elvis earned the respect of his outfit. They felt he was a regular fellow and tried to protect him from his fans.

I hear the communists in East Germany have arrested a "gang." It's called "The Elvis Presley Hound Dogs."

Elvis differed from the other GIs when it came to mail call. He received as many as 10,000 letters a week. Most of them were sent on to the Colonel.

Elvis and his father Vernon met their future wives in Germany: Priscilla Beaulieu and Davada (Dee) Stanley. Priscilla, the daughter of an air force captain stationed in Germany, was fourteen when Elvis met her.

Sergeant Elvis Presley was honorably discharged from the army in March 1960. He flew from Germany to McGuire Air Force Base in New Jersey. He arrived at 6:35 a.m. in a blinding snowstorm. He was greeted by hundreds of fans, the press, the Colonel, and friends.

I understand you received a Certificate of Achievement for faithful duty and service.

Frank Sinatra's daughter Nancy presented him with a gift of dress shirts from her father.

While he was in the army there were many takeoffs of Elvis and his style.

On a TV show, Phil Silvers sang "You're Nothing but A Raccoon," and "Brown Suede Combat Boots."

Bye Bye Birdie, a Broadway show about a rock 'n' roll singer named Birdie, ran for two years.

The Colonel had made sure that Elvis' name had remained well known.

Elvis made two million dollars in 1958 and even more in 1959.

A BIG HUNK O' LOVE
MY WISH COME TRUE
A DATE WITH ELVIS
KING CREOLE

ELVIS

ELVIS WE LOVE YOU

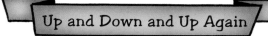

Up and Down and Up Again

Out of the army, Elvis' career again went into high gear—but with some changes. There were no more sideburns and no hard rock music. A more mature Elvis sang romantic ballads.

The whole way from Memphis, twenty-four hours a day, the fans have been lining the tracks.

Elvis stopped for a few days at Graceland, his old home. Then he left by train for Miami Beach to do a TV special with Frank Sinatra.

We have here the idols of two generations. Man, that's history.

Elvis received $125,000 for a six minute guest shot on the Sinatra special.

In 1961 Elvis gave two sellout benefit performances in Memphis and one in Hawaii. Jimmy Stewart and Minnie Pearl had been on the plane too, but the 25,000 fans were there to see Elvis.

That was his last concert until 1969. But Elvis continued to make box office hit movies—*G.I. Blues, Flaming Star, Blue Hawaii.*

From the spring of 1962 to the winter of 1969 Elvis didn't have any number one songs.

ELVIS Fe
ELVIS lovin'
ELVIS swing

ELVIS PRESLEY ...in two roles for the first time!

KISSIN' COUSINS

The Colonel saw to it that the movies continued to make money. But neither Elvis' singing nor acting talent was used.

Kissin' Cousins was the first "quickie" movie. It was shot in seventeen days to save money. The quickie movies that followed were poorly made.

Because he could never appear in public without being mobbed, Elvis kept his Memphis Mafia for protection and companionship. They were old friends from his youth and a few army buddies.

How many young men does Elvis have on his staff?

How do you really feel about Elvis?

Sometimes seven, sometimes as many as twelve.

They played football, swam, rode motorcycles. His friends said he was polite, generous, and full of fun.

We love him like a big brother. We try to keep him happy—even when he loses his temper. He feels down sometimes, but we understand.

In 1960 Priscilla Beaulieu flew over from Germany to spend Christmas with Elvis, his father Vernon, and his stepmother Dee.

I sure like this better than last year in the army. And Dee, I'm real glad Dad married you.

At her father's request, Priscilla stayed at Graceland with Vernon, Dee, Elvis' grandmother, and aunt.

Priscilla finished high school in 1963 and then went on to study modeling.

You see before you, the true Hollywood boy.

Ha Ha.

Elvis spent most of his time in Hollywood making movies.

For years the newspaper gossip columns and movie magazines linked Elvis' name with one starlet after another.

But on May 1, 1967, in Las Vegas, Elvis Presley married Priscilla Beaulieu.

The wedding ceremony may have been small—just family. But the reception was staged by the Colonel for the press.

Elvis and Priscilla, without the Memphis Mafia, spent much of their time at Circle G, a 163-acre ranch near Graceland.

It will be hard to leave all this to go back to Hollywood and work.

Their daughter, Lisa Marie, was born February 1, 1968. Elvis was never happier.

Calls are coming in from all over the world!

And guards are on duty to keep the fans away!

But Elvis couldn't settle down to married life. Priscilla, with Lisa Marie, left him in 1972—and the Memphis Mafia, his friends, moved back in.

Elvis made no public appearances from 1962 to mid 1969. Many of his fans switched to the younger stars: Bob Dylan, the Beatles, the Rolling Stones, Jefferson Airplane.

I'm still loyal to Elvis!

Well, I'm a fan of the Beatles.

Gosh, isn't he wonderful?

I'm getting tired of his movies. They're all alike.

Then in December 1968 Elvis made a TV special.

NBC has a smash hit. Lucky for Elvis they talked the Colonel out of the usual Christmas show.

And that song "If I Can Dream" is going straight to the top in sales. It will be a great hit.

In July 1969 Elvis appeared in person at the International Hotel in Las Vegas. Fans came from all over the world to see him. He was again on top.

I came from England.

I came from even further, from Australia.

From then on Elvis appeared in Las Vegas for one month in the winter and one month in the summer—for one million dollars a month. He appeared at the Houston Astrodome for one million dollars a show.

His appearances in the '70s in Las Vegas, the Houston Astrodome, and Madison Square Garden in New York were sellouts. But Elvis was beginning to have problems.

He gave Pricilla a big settlement.

In 1973 Elvis and Pricilla were divorced.

His hair is gray now. He dyes it black.

Elvis had a weight problem. He was getting fat. Sometimes he wouldn't allow any pictures to be taken of him.

Elvis is tired out. He used to love to perform. Now it's hard work for him.

He has several health problems. He doesn't smoke or drink—but he does overeat.

On August 16, 1977, Elvis Presley died of a heart attack. He was 42-years-old.

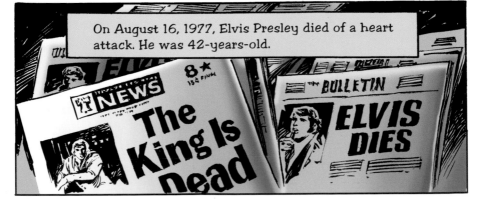

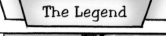

The Legend

Something is wrong. Every time I open an engagement Elvis sends me a guitar made of flowers. It hasn't come.

Ann-Margret made a movie with Elvis. They remained friends. When hearing of his death, she talked about him during her Las Vegas performance.

We lost a good friend today.

Sinatra dedicated his concert to Elvis. Many other stars of stage and screen paid tribute to him.

Memphis lowered its flags to half-mast. Phone calls came in from all over the world, more than the system could handle.

President Carter praised Elvis as a symbol of the country's vitality, rebelliousness, and good humor.

And over 100,000 fans went to Graceland to pay tribute. The country mourned his loss.

Elvis had been king, and like other famous people, had a lot of gossip written about him.

Some of the newspaper stories didn't agree with the facts.

The medical examiner has found no signs of drug abuse.

He was engaged to the lovely Ginger Alden. He was happy.

At the time of his death, Elvis had a hit record. His current concert tour had been sold out.

He was happy. He loved nice things, showy things, especially cars.

And he loved to be generous with his family, his friends, and charities.

Elvis made 33 movies. He had 45 records that sold over one million each. He was born the son of a sharecropper, but he died a multimillionaire.

He changed the direction of American pop music. Elvis Presley was an American legend.

Saddleback's Graphic Fiction & Nonfiction

If you enjoyed this Graphic Biography ... you will also enjoy our other graphic titles including:

Graphic Classics

- Around the World in Eighty Days
- The Best of Poe
- Black Beauty
- The Call of the Wild
- A Christmas Carol
- A Connecticut Yankee in King Arthur's Court
- Dr. Jekyll and Mr. Hyde
- Dracula
- Frankenstein
- The Great Adventures of
- Sherlock Holmes
- Gulliver's Travels
- Huckleberry Finn
- The Hunchback of Notre Dame
- The Invisible Man
- Jane Eyre
- Journey to the Center of the Earth
- Kidnapped
- The Last of the Mohicans
- The Man in the Iron Mask
- Moby Dick
- The Mutiny On Board H.M.S. Bounty
- The Mysterious Island
- The Prince and the Pauper
- The Red Badge of Courage
- The Scarlet Letter
- The Swiss Family Robinson
- A Tale of Two Cities
- The Three Musketeers
- The Time Machine
- Tom Sawyer
- Treasure Island
- 20,000 Leagues Under the Sea
- The War of the Worlds

Graphic Shakespeare

- As You Like It
- Hamlet
- Julius Caesar
- King Lear
- Macbeth
- The Merchant of Venice
- A Midsummer Night's Dream
- Othello
- Romeo and Juliet
- The Taming of the Shrew
- The Tempest
- Twelfth Night

SADDLEBACK
EDUCATIONAL PUBLISHING